Dear Parent:
Your child's love of reading starts here!

Every child learns to read in a different way and at his or her own speed. Some go back and forth between reading levels and read favorite books again and again. Others read through each level in order. You can help your young reader improve and become more confident by encouraging his or her own interests and abilities. From books your child reads with you to the first books he or she reads alone, there are I Can Read Books for every stage of reading:

SHARED READING
Basic language, word repetition, and whimsical illustrations, ideal for sharing with your emergent reader

BEGINNING READING
Short sentences, familiar words, and simple concepts for children eager to read on their own

READING WITH HELP
Engaging stories, longer sentences, and language play for developing readers

READING ALONE
Complex plots, challenging vocabulary, and high-interest topics for the independent reader

ADVANCED READING
Short paragraphs, chapters, and exciting themes for the perfect bridge to chapter books

I Can Read Books have introduced children to the joy of reading since 1957. Featuring award-winning authors and illustrators and a fabulous cast of beloved characters, I Can Read Books set the standard for beginning readers.

A lifetime of discovery begins with the magical words **"I Can Read!"**

Visit www.icanread.com for information
on enriching your child's reading experience.

Pinkalicious®
and the Pinkatastic Zoo Day

For Megan!
xox,
Aunt Victoria

The author gratefully acknowledges
the artistic and editorial contributions
of Daniel Griffo and Natalie Engel.

I Can Read Book® is a trademark of HarperCollins Publishers.

Pinkalicious and the Pinkatastic Zoo Day
Copyright © 2012 by Victoria Kann

PINKALICIOUS and all related logos and characters are trademarks of Victoria Kann. Used with permission.

Library of Congress catalog card number: 2011963517
ISBN 978-0-06-218780-2 (trade bdg.) — ISBN 978-0-06-218779-6 (pbk.)

12 13 14 15 16 LP/WOR 10 9 8 7 6 5 4 3 2 1
❖
First Edition

Pinkalicious®
and the Pinkatastic Zoo Day

by Victoria Kann

HARPER
An Imprint of HarperCollinsPublishers

One sunny Saturday,

I squeezed my teddy bear tight.

"Guess what, Henrietta," I said.

"It's Teddy Bear Day at the zoo!"

"I'm bringing Fred," said Peter.

7

At the zoo, we walked by the zebras.

"These guys could use

a hint of pink," I said to myself.

I waved my wand and pink-a-presto!

A zebra changed the color of

its stripes.

"Pink!" I waved my wand at the lions.

The hippos and rhinos came next.

"Pink! Pink!" I commanded.

"What are you doing, Pinkalicious?"

asked Peter.

I waved my wand at him, too.

Then I remembered the teddy bear picnic.

I love teddy bears and picnics!

Peter and I gave Fred and Henrietta
teddy-back rides down the path.
The Teddy Bear Day fun was starting!
We got bear-shaped balloons.

We spread out a large blanket.

We sipped honey tea

and ate teddy bear cookies.

Peter gave Fred a sip of tea, too.

"Fred says this tea is BEARY good,"

said Peter.

I couldn't wait to see
the real bears,
but when we got to the bears
they were all sleeping.
It was boring to watch.

"Pinkalicious!" Peter pointed.

I looked up and gasped.

Above us, a vine led from

the monkey house to a field.

One monkey was crossing over!

The little monkey

did tricks on the vine.

She swung from side to side.

She hung upside down by her tail.

I didn't want Henrietta to miss out,
so Daddy put her on his shoulder.

I saw the monkey look at Henrietta.

She clapped her hands and hooted.

I had a funny feeling that something

bad was about to happen.

18

"Oh, no!" I cried
as the monkey swung down low.
She scooped up Henrietta!
"Well I'll be a monkey's uncle,"
Daddy said, amazed.

I watched as the monkey
scurried over to the field.
"She thinks Henrietta is
her teddy bear," Peter said.

The monkey rocked Henrietta
and gave her a big hug.
Peter laughed.
But I didn't think it was funny.
Not one little bit.

I tried everything to get the monkey

to bring Henrietta back.

I sang to her.

I made silly faces at her.

I even asked Peter to try

speaking in monkey to her.

Nothing worked!

She kept on playing with Henrietta.

"You're making a monkey

out of my teddy bear!" I said.

"I'm sorry, Pinkalicious,"
said Mommy.
"The zoo is closing.
We have to go."

"Oh, no! This is unbearable.

What about Henrietta?" I said.

I started to cry.

"We'll think of something,"

Daddy promised.

I didn't know what else to do.

At home, all I could think about
was poor Henrietta.
I loved her so much.
How could I explain that
to a monkey?

Suddenly, I had an idea.

"Quick, Peter," I said.

I told him my plan.

We got right to work.

The next day,

we got to the zoo bright and early.

I found the little monkey right away.

"I have a gift for you," I said.

I held up the snuggly sock monkey

that Peter and I had made.

"Now watch me," I told the monkey.

I gave the new toy a squeeze.

The monkey hugged Henrietta.

I patted the sock monkey's head.

The little monkey patted Henrietta.

I tossed the sock monkey into the field.

The monkey tossed Henrietta over to me!

I picked up my teddy bear
and the little monkey
picked up her new friend.

"Good-bye!" I waved.

"It was fun monkeying around
with you!"